WITHDRAWN

2 4 APR 2022

Z is

for Moose

BY KELLY BINGHAM

PICTURES BY PAUL O. ZELINSKY

ANDERSEN PRESS

Z is for Moose by Kelly Bingham and Paul O. Zelinsky
Text copyright © 2012 by Kelly Bingham.
Illustration copyright © 2012 by Paul O. Zelinksy.
Originally published by Greenwillow Books, an imprint
of HarperCollins Publishers USA
Published by arrangement with Pippin Properties, Inc.
through Rights People, London.

This paperback edition first published in 2013
by Andersen Press Ltd.,
20 Vauxhall Bridge Road, London SW1V 2SA.
Published in Australia by Random House Australia Pty.,
Level 3, 100 Pacific Highway, North Sydney, NSW 2060.

10 9 8 7 6 5 4 3 2

British Library Cataloguing in Publication Data available.

ISBN 978 1 84939 781 0

For Sam, who asked for a funny book,
and for Benny, because I love you too. K.B.

♥ is for Rachel. P. O. Z.

A is for Apple

B is for Ball

C is for Cat

E is for Elephant

F is for Fox

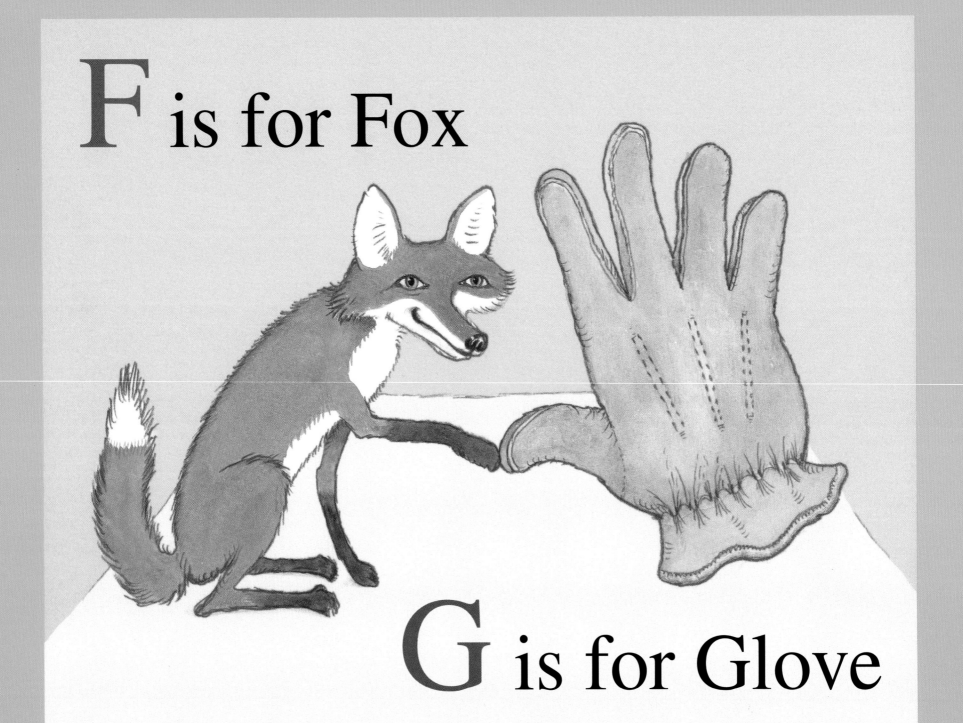

G is for Glove

I is for Ice Cream

J is for Jar

K is for Kangaroo

L is for Lollipop

N is for Needle

T is for Truck

U is for Umbrella

V is for Violin

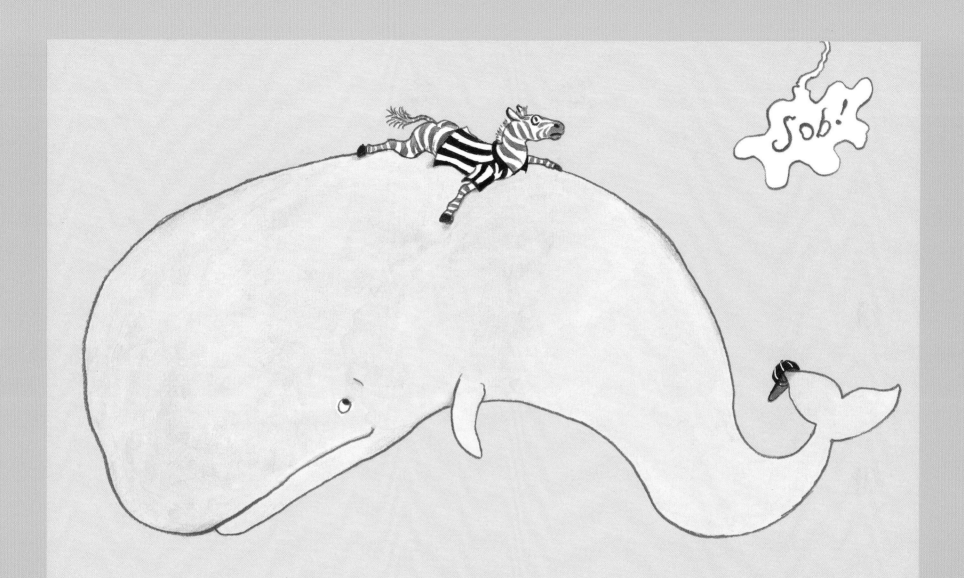

W is for Whale

X is for Xylophone

Z is for
Zebra's friend, Moose